READING Makes You Feel Good

Todd PARR

LITTLE, BROWN AND COMPANY

New York Boston

To my Grandma Logan, who introduced me to
Green Eggs and Ham,
I Love you very much,
Todd

Little, Brown and Company

Hachette Book Group
1290 Avenue of the Americas, New York, NY 10104
Visit our website at www.lb-kids.com

Little, Brown and Company is a division of Hachette Book Group, Inc.
The Little, Brown name and logo are trademarks of Hachette Book Group, Inc.

The publisher is not responsible for websites (or their content) that are not owned by the publisher.

First Paperback Edition: April 2009
First published in hardcover in June 2005 by Little, Brown and Company

Library of Congress Cataloging-in-Publication Data

Parr, Todd.
    Reading makes you feel good / Todd Parr. — 1st ed.
    p. cm.
"Megan Tingley Books"
Summary: Describes the characteristics and various advantages of reading.
[1. Books and Reading—Fiction.] I. Title
PZ7 P2447 Re 2005
[E]—dc22   2004010274
ISBN 978-0-316-16004-9 (hc) / ISBN 978-0-316-04348-9 (pb)

10

Imago

Printed in China

Reading makes you feel good because....

You can imagine you are a brave

princess or a scary dinosaur

You can learn about

You can make

a new friend

And you can do it anywhere!

to make pizza

animal at the zoo

You can make someone feel

You can learn how to

book with anyone

And you can

BOOK

do it anywhere!

Reading is important! When you read or when someone reads to you it helps you learn and discover new things. Curl up with someone special and read a book. You'll feel really good.
Love,
Todd

P.S. See if you can read all the words I put in the pictures!